the CRITTER club

Ellie's Lovely Idea

by Callie Barkley 💜 illustrated by Marsha Riti

LITTLE SIMON

New York London Toronto Sydney New Delhi

LITTLE SIMON

An imprint of Simon & Schuster Children's Publishing Division 1230 Avenue of the Americas, New York, New York 10020 Copyright © 2013 by Simon & Schuster, Inc. All rights reserved, including the right of reproduction in whole or in part in any form. LITTLE SIMON is a registered trademark of Simon & Schuster, Inc., and associated colophon is a trademark of Simon & Schuster, Inc. For information about special discounts for bulk purchases, please contact Simon & Schuster Special Sales at 1-866-506-1949 or business@simonandschuster.com. The Simon & Schuster Speakers Bureau can bring authors to your live event. For more information or to book an event contact the Simon & Schuster Speakers Bureau at 1-866-248-3049 or visit our website at www.simonspeakers.com. Designed by Laura Roode.
Manufactured in the United States of America 1113 FFG
First Edition 10 9 8 7 6 5 4 3 2 1
Library of Congress Cataloging-in-Publication Data
Barkley, Callie. Ellie's lovely idea / by Callie Barkley ; illustrated by Marsha Riti. — First edition. pages cm — (Critter club ; #6) Summary: Valentine's Day is near, and to raise money for a charity called Puppy Love, Ellie persuades the other Critter Club girls to join her in selling and delivering singing telegrams. [1. Fund raising—Fiction. 2. Best friends—Fiction. 3. Friendship—Fiction. 4. Singing—Fiction. 5. Valentine's Day—Fiction.] I. Riti, Marsha, illustrator. II. Title. PZ7.B250585Ell 2013 [Fic]—dc23 2012049764
ISBN 978-1-4424-8218-0 (pbk)
ISBN 978-1-4424-8219-7 (hc)
ISBN 978-1-4424-8220-3 (eBook)

Table of Contents

Chapter 1

Love Is in the Air

Early on a Saturday morning, Ellie and her three best friends, Liz, Marion, and Amy, were making valentines in Amy's kitchen. The girls had slept over at Amy's house. They were still in their pajamas!

"Ten down, ten to go!" Ellie said, adding a valentine to her DONE pile. She smiled. Ellie loved seeing her name in red glitter!

Valentine's Day was next Friday— less than a week away! There would be  a party in their second-grade class. The girls were making valentines to give to their classmates.

"Valentine's Day is so much

fun," said Liz as she finished up her second valentine. Liz was a true artist. She was taking lots of time on each card.

"Me too," Marion said. "February would be so boring without it." Marion was using lots of ribbon.

3

Each one of her cards looked like an award. Marion knew all about winning awards. She was really good at piano and ballet and a great horseback rider.

"It *has* been a quiet month," said Amy. She was cutting and folding her cards into tiny books. "We haven't had any animals at the Critter Club for weeks!"

The Critter Club was the animal shelter that the four girls had started in their town of Santa Vista. Their friend Ms. Sullivan had come up with the idea after the girls had found her missing puppy. Ms. Sullivan had even let them take over her empty barn. Now it was the Critter Club! With the help of Amy's mom, who was a veterinarian, the girls cared for stray, lost, or hurt animals.

"That reminds me!" cried Amy. "We got a photo from the woman who adopted Penny." Penny was a stray Dalmatian that the girls had been taking care of—until a few weeks ago. Together they had found the perfect home for her.

Amy got the photo from the kitchen.

Ellie sighed. "I sure do miss having her around the Critter Club." Amy, Liz, and Marion all nodded.

Just then, Amy's mom, Dr. Purvis, came in from the living room. "I couldn't help overhearing you girls while I was opening the mail," she said. "You know, just because there are no animals at the club doesn't mean you can't help some *other* animals."

Dr. Purvis dropped an open envelope onto the table. Then she winked and walked away.

Ellie reached for the envelope. She pulled out the paper inside. Amy, Liz, and

Marion looked over her shoulder.

"Oh! Puppy Love!" said Amy. "This is an organization that my mom's friend Rebecca started. That's her." Amy pointed to the woman in the photo. "She gives money to families who need help paying for their new puppy's

medical care—like all the shots that keep a puppy healthy."

"It looks like Puppy Love is try-ing to raise more money," Marion pointed out.

Ellie looked at the cute puppies in the photo and smiled. *How much* money do I have at home in my piggy bank? she wondered. *Twelve dollars?* She would gladly donate it all to Puppy Love to help those families— and puppies—who needed it.

I just wish it could be more, she thought. *Much, much more.*

chapter 2

A Musical Idea

Ellie and her nana Gloria carried bowls of popcorn into the family room. It was Saturday night—movie night—at Ellie's house. But her parents had gone out to dinner and her little brother, Toby, was upstairs reading.

"Guess it's just us tonight, Nana," Ellie said with a smile. Watching

old movies with her grand-
mother was one of her
favorite things to do.

"Just us! Just
us!" squawked
Lenny the parrot
from his perch in the
corner. Lenny belonged
to Nana Gloria. Together
they had come to live
with Ellie's family.

Ellie laughed. "You too, Lenny!"

"What movie are we watching
tonight?" Nana Gloria asked.

"Ms. Sullivan lent it to me,"

Ellie said. "It's called *The Singing Telegram*. And the star of it is Ruby Fairchild—your favorite!"

As Nana Gloria clapped, Ellie smiled a secret smile. She was the only one who knew that Ms. Sullivan had once been known as the famous Hollywood actress Ruby Fairchild.

That was years and years ago. Now Ms. Sullivan wanted to have a quiet life in Santa Vista. Her secret was safe with Ellie.

Ellie sat next to Nana Gloria and pressed play on the remote.

Like all of Ruby Fairchild's movies, this one was black and white.

The movie was about a shy young man who falls in love with a young woman. The only time he feels

sure of himself is when he is sing-ing. So he gets a job as a telegram deliveryman. One day he delivers a singing telegram to the woman he

loves, telling her of his feelings. But he doesn't say who it's from. By the end of the movie, she figures it out and they live happily ever after.

Ellie loved every moment. Lenny seemed to like it too. "Bravo! Bravo! *Squawk!*" he cried as the closing song played. Ellie giggled. She had taught Lenny to say "Bravo!" when she sang, which she did a lot. Now he said it whenever he heard any music.

"Did people really send tele-grams back then?" Ellie wanted to know.

Nana Gloria nodded. "Oh, yes," she said. "Way before cell phones and e-mail, people sent them all the time."

"Nana, have *you* ever gotten a *singing* telegram?" Ellie asked.

"I have!" Nana Gloria replied with a smile. "I'll never forget it. Your grandfather sent me one for

my birthday once. It was one of the best presents I've ever gotten."

Ellie giggled. "It sounds like such a fun way to show your love . . ." She trailed off. An idea was quickly forming in her head: herself, Ellie, plus singing, plus delivering messages of love and friendship. It all added up to . . . singing telegrams for Valentine's Day! *That's something I'd do just for fun!* Ellie thought. *But maybe people would make a small donation to Puppy Love to have their message delivered. Then it would be for a good cause, too!*

Now if only she could just get Liz, Marion, and Amy to go along with the idea. . . .

Chapter 3

Singers for Hire

"I can't believe we're doing this," Amy said nervously.

"Ellie, are you sure we're ready?" Liz asked.

"Yeah," added Marion. "Maybe we need a few more practices?"

The girls were backstage in the school auditorium. In front of the curtain, the whole school was filing in for Monday morning assembly.

Ellie pulled her friends into a little huddle. "You guys," she said excitedly, "this is a great way to advertise our singing telegram service."

The day before, Sunday, Ellie had invited the girls over. She had explained her idea to raise money for Puppy Love. They had all agreed it was a great idea. Liz had even made some posters to hang up at school.

Show Your Love

Singing Telegram Service for Valentine's Day!
$5 each, profits go to Puppy Love

Just tell us who the telegram is for and what kind of message you'd like to send. We'll write a one-of-a-kind song just for them and deliver it by Valentine's Day!

There was just one thing they didn't agree on. "Tell us again," said Marion. "Why can't *you* deliver the singing telegrams on your *own*?"

"You're such a great singer," Liz told Ellie.

"And so good onstage," added Amy. "Some of us . . . aren't."

Ellie beamed. She was enjoying her friends' nice words. But she also knew she and her friends would sound better all together.

"Come on," Ellie said. "It'll be fun

to sing together. And won't it feel more special for the person who is getting the telegram?"

Amy shrugged. Liz nodded. Marion smiled a tiny smile.

"Okay, then," said Ellie. "Let's do this!"

She peeked around the curtain. They just needed to wait for the sign from the principal, Mrs. Young. Ellie had worked everything out with her. Mrs. Young had only one rule: The girls couldn't deliver the singing telegrams during school hours. But she let them hang up the posters all around school. There was also a drop box in the hallway for telegram order forms and money.

Mrs. Young was announcing them. "Students," she was saying, "first up, we have a special treat. Four of our second-grade students are helping to raise money for a great charity called Puppy Love. They will be delivering singing telegrams for Valentine's Day!"

Mrs. Young waved to Ellie.

"That's our sign," whispered Ellie. She led the girls out onto the stage. Ellie took her place front and center. Liz, Marion, and Amy lined up behind her.

And then they began to sing, just as they'd practiced.

L-O-V, add an E,
That spells LOVE and love is free.
But for just five dollars, you can send
A musical note to your best friend!

Tell us who, tell us where,
Tell us when and we'll be there.
Tell us what to say, we'll turn it into song,
Show your love, you won't go wrong!

Ellie beamed as she sang. Her friends' voices blended beautifully behind her. For Ellie, it was over all too soon. The audience was clapping, and the girls were walking offstage. *I knew we should have*

practiced a third verse, she thought.

After the assembly, the four friends walked to their classroom together. "That was so great!" Ellie said excitedly.

"I don't know," said Amy uncertainly. "I messed up at least twice."

"I didn't even notice," said Liz, putting an arm around Amy.

"Me neither," said Marion. "I actually think we *did* sound good. Delivering singing telegrams could be really fun . . . *if* anyone signs up, that is."

DONATIONS
♡ GO TO ♡
♡ PUPPY LOVE ♡

At lunchtime that day, the girls walked past the drop box in the hallway. Ellie couldn't resist. She peeked under the lid.

"Well?" said Liz at her side. "Are there any orders?"

Ellie looked up, her eyes wide. She lifted the lid. The box was already half full! More than twenty people had already signed up to send a singing telegram!

Amy gasped, very surprised. Marion's jaw dropped.

Ellie clapped. "And we're just getting started!" she exclaimed. "Girls, we are in business!"

Chapter 4

Special Deliveries!

After school, the girls met up at Marion's house. They had a lot of work to do!

"Today is Monday," said Marion. She had her clipboard out. She started making a list. "We could start delivering telegrams tomorrow after school. Let's say we deliver about five a day. We can get them

all done by Friday afternoon—
Valentine's Day."

"We might get more orders!"
Ellie pointed out.

Liz nodded. "We'll have to fit
them in somehow," she said.

The group agreed to meet up
every day after school that week.

Then they got started on some tele-grams to be delivered the next day.

Amy loved writing poems, so she wrote the words to the song.

Marion decided on the tune of the music. She stuck to easy tunes, like "Happy Birthday" and "Row, Row, Row Your Boat."

Liz decorated a copy of the lyrics. The girls would give it to the person who received the telegram—as a Valentine's Day card.

Then Ellie led the girls in a rehearsal. They practiced singing each telegram a few times.

Soon they had ten singing tele-grams, all ready to go. They took a break and had some hot cocoa.

"I can't wait to see the look on

the first person's face!" Ellie said eagerly. "What a fun surprise!"

On Tuesday after school Dr. Purvis dropped the girls off at the first address. She had offered to drive them from place to place. She

waited in the car while the girls went up to the front door.

"Everybody ready?" asked Ellie as she rang the doorbell.

Liz, Amy, and Marion nodded. They huddled around the lyric sheet. Within moments a dark-haired fifth grader opened the door.

"Hi!" said Ellie. "You're Rosie, right?"

The girl nodded.

"Then this is for you!" cried Ellie.

All together the girls started to sing.

Telegram For You! ♡

Ro, Ro, Rosie Cho
from my soccer team,
I hope you have a
great Valentine's Day!
From your friend,
Eileen

Rosie clapped and smiled. "Oh, that's soooo nice!" she said. "Thank you!"

Then Liz handed her the lyric-sheet valentine. "Happy Valentine's Day!" she said.

And just like that, the girls had delivered their first singing telegram. They walked together down Rosie's front walk.

"Wow," said Amy. "That was kind of fun!"

"Did you see how happy she was?" said Liz.

"Where to next?" asked Ellie eagerly.

Marion checked her clipboard. Off they went to the next address, a block away. The second telegram was for a first-grade teacher from her students. It was a valentine *and* get-well message.

♡ Telegram For You! ♡

Mrs. West, Mrs. West,
Your foot really needs
a rest.
While you're out,
we'll try our very best
on this Friday's
spelling test.
From, Your Students

A+

"Wonderful!" Mrs. West cheered. "You girls are fantastic! And so are my first graders."

The girls were on a roll. They delivered three more telegrams.

Then Marion checked her watch.
"How about one more for today?"
she said.

The others agreed. Dr. Purvis drove them to the last house of the day. Ellie rang the doorbell. A woman Nana Gloria's age answered the door.

"Hello!" said Ellie. "We have a singing telegram for Grandma Sue. It's from your grandchildren!"

Telegram for You!
We love you, Grandma Sue.
We know you've been feeling blue.
We'll help you
decide what to do
to cheer up your
Princess Boo.

The girls finished their song. Unlike the others, Grandma Sue did not clap. She did not smile. She didn't say anything.

She started to cry.

Ellie looked at her friends. A terrible thought flashed through her mind. *Oh no. Did we really sound that bad?*

Ellie Meets a Princess

"That was lovely," Grandma Sue said at last, wiping her tears. "Thank you so much." She sniffed. "I'm sorry about all my crying. I've just been so very worried about my princess, that's all."

"Your princess?" Ellie said.

"Yes, my Princess Boo," said Grandma Sue. "She's my pet

lovebird. She's not well."

"*Awww,*" the girls said in unison.

Grandma Sue nodded. She explained that Princess Boo had seemed off lately. She wasn't eating much. Grandma Sue feared she was getting sick.

Ellie and the other girls looked at one another. *A sick animal?* Ellie thought. *Sounds like our thing!*

Ellie spoke up. "Amy's mom is a veterinarian," she said. "Would you like her to take a look at Princess Boo right now?"

Grandma Sue's eyes went wide. "Oh, would she?" she asked.

Amy nodded. "I'm sure she would be happy to!" she said.

The girls were right. Dr. Purvis was more than happy to help. Within minutes, she was giving Princess Boo a quick checkup in Grandma Sue's living room. The girls and Grandma Sue looked on.

Princess Boo was a beautiful green bird with some pink and red around her beak and on her neck, and a bit of blue on her tail.

"Well, Dr. Purvis?" Grandma Sue

asked after a bit. "What's wrong with my princess?"

Dr. Purvis put Princess Boo back on her perch. "Nothing," she said. "At least, not medically. But I have

some questions. Does anyone else live with you, besides Princess Boo?"

Grandma Sue shook her head. "No, it's just the two of us."

"And how much of the day are you home?" Dr. Purvis asked.

Grandma Sue thought it over. "Well, I have a part-time job on

weekdays," she said. "Three eve-
nings a week I go to my book
club. On weekends, I do errands.
Sometimes I go on long walks with
my friend. Otherwise I'm home.
Why do you ask?"

Dr. Purvis nodded. "I
think I know what's
wrong," she said.
"Princess Boo

might have a case of . . . loneliness."

"Loneliness?" said the girls and Grandma Sue all together.

Dr. Purvis explained that most lovebirds needed companionship. She said they were happiest when someone could be with them much of the day. "Some lovebird owners have *two* of them," she said. "That way the birds keep each other company."

"Oh!" cried Grandma Sue. Her face brightened. "So I should get another bird!"

"Well," Dr. Purvis said, "first, I have an idea. Maybe Princess Boo could spend time with someone else's bird. See how it goes. If it seems to help her feel better"—Dr. Purvis smiled—"then you'll know if it's a good idea to get another bird."

Grandma Sue nodded. "That's a smart idea," she said. "There's just one problem. I don't know anyone else who has a bird."

Ellie felt her friends' eyes on her. She was already way ahead of them.

"I do!" Ellie cried.

Chapter 6

Bird Buddies

Liz, Amy, and Marion had just arrived at Ellie's house. It was Wednesday after school. The girls were going to write a few more telegrams. Then they'd head out to deliver some, too.

"I think Princess Boo is looking better already!" said Liz with a smile.

Princess Boo was inside her cage, which was right next to Lenny's perch.

"Grandma Sue dropped her off this morning," Ellie said. "She'll pick her up after dinner tonight."

Amy giggled. "It will be like a bird playdate!"

"Yep!" Ellie replied. "And I think she'll come again tomorrow.

Nana Gloria said they got along very well all day today."

"Very well! Very well!" squawked Lenny.

"See?" Ellie said, laughing with her friends.

The girls started on the telegrams. As usual, Amy got to work writing the words. Marion checked the address list. Liz sharpened her colored pencils.

Ellie had nothing to do until they were ready to practice. She let her mind wander. She thought about the people they had surprised the day before. They were all so happy! *It must feel great to get such a special surprise. I wish someone would send me a telegram!* she thought. She imagined it: the doorbell ringing, the surprise of seeing the girls there, singing a special song just for her.

Who would it be from? A secret admirer? A friend? And what would the message be?

"I was just thinking," Ellie said out loud to her friends. "What if someone wanted to send one of *us* a telegram?"

Amy looked up from her notebook. "One of us?" she asked.

Ellie nodded. "Yeah. Like, let's say, me. Just for example. How would that work?"

Liz smiled. "Hmm," she said. "You mean, how would we keep it secret? If the telegram were for you?"

"Right," said Ellie. "So that it would be a surprise for me. Or for any one of us."

Marion tapped her pencil eraser against her chin. "I'm sure we could figure something out," she said with a sneaky smile. "Why do you ask, Ellie?"

"Oh . . . uh!" said Ellie, "no reason." *No way*

am I going to ask them to send me a telegram, she thought. *That wouldn't be the same as someone sending it on their own.*

Ellie was quiet for a minute. Then she asked, "So no one has . . . ordered a telegram . . . for any of us?"

Marion shook her head. "Nope," she said. "Not yet."

chapter 7

Lenny the Chatterbox

By Thursday afternoon the girls were getting a little bit tired. Meeting each day after school took up a lot of time.

And Ellie still had to squeeze in her chores—like walking their dog. Sam, their golden retriever, loved long strolls. But Ellie's friends were back at her house, writing

telegrams. She wanted to get back.

"Come on, Sam," she said. "Can we walk a little faster?"

But Sam wouldn't head home the short way. He pulled at the leash until Ellie let him walk on.

They went all the way around the block.

By the time they got home, the girls were putting on their coats.

"We're finished!" said Amy. "Everything's ready for tomorrow!"

Ellie was confused. "But . . . don't we have some to deliver?" she asked.

"Nope," said Liz. "The only ones left are the telegrams that people want delivered tomorrow— on Valentine's Day."

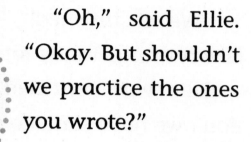

"Oh," said Ellie. "Okay. But shouldn't we practice the ones you wrote?"

"We did!" said Marion. "And you're so good at singing, you hardly need practice." She patted Ellie on the back. "I have to get home to do my homework."

"Me too," said Amy.

"Me three," said Liz. "Bye, Ellie!"

In a flash they were out the front door and gone.

Ellie stood frozen to her spot. "Well, they left in a hurry," she remarked.

Ellie took off Sam's leash. Then she went in to see Lenny. Next to him, Princess Boo was squawking cheerfully in her cage.

"I missed all the fun!" Ellie said to the birds.

"All the fun! *Squawk!*" said Lenny.

Ellie sighed. She flopped onto the sofa. "It's all Sam's fault. He sure was taking his time."

"Taking his time! Taking his time!" Lenny squawked. Then all of a sudden, he added: "Ellie's favorite song! Favorite song!"

Ellie looked up at him. "What?" she said.

"What? *Squawk!* What?" Lenny echoed.

Ellie stood up and walked over

to Lenny's perch. "No, before that. Did you say 'Ellie's favorite song'?"

"Ellie's favorite song! *Squawk!*"

"Yes! Yes!" Ellie cried. "You *did*! But . . . why?"

Ellie knew that parrots like Lenny could mimic. That meant they could copy words or sounds they heard. "But I didn't say those words," said Ellie. "You must have heard them from someone else."

"Someone else! *Squawk!*" Lenny screeched.

Then it hit her. *The girls!* she thought. *The girls were just in here. They were working on telegrams.*

Why would they be talking about my favorite song?

Everyone knew Ellie's favorite song was "Take Me Out to the Ball Game." Ellie's family loved going to baseball games. She dreamed of singing that song at a big-league game someday.

But why would the girls talk about that while writing telegrams? Ellie wondered.

There was only one explanation that made sense to her.

I'm getting a telegram tomorrow!

Chapter 8

Ready, Set, Surprise!

Ellie looked in the mirror. She practiced her happy, surprised face. *Perfect!* she thought. *I don't want to look like I was expecting a telegram.*

She checked her outfit: her red wrap sweater, red skirt with sequins, and pink leggings.

Ellie felt ready for Valentine's Day. And she was *definitely* ready to be surprised!

I just wonder when *they'll deliver my telegram,* she thought on her walk to school.

Their teacher, Mrs. Sienna, had planned their classroom party for the morning. Everyone in class had a valentine mailbox—a decorated paper bag taped to each desk. The kids walked around the classroom to deliver their valentines.

Liz, Marion, and Amy came up to Ellie.

"Ellie," said Marion with a big smile, "we have something for you."

This is it! thought Ellie. *They're going to deliver my singing telegram now. How exciting!*

Liz was reaching into her back-pack. "We all worked on it together," she said.

"We hope you like it," added Marion.

Ellie got ready to flash her happy, surprised face. Liz handed her a heart-shaped card.

Ellie looked at it quickly, then up at her friends, expecting the singing to begin.

But it didn't. Liz, Marion, and Amy just stood there smiling.

That's when Ellie realized: It was just a valentine— not a singing telegram.

"Oh!" said Ellie. She tried hard not to look disappointed. "What an awesome valentine. You guys are so sweet.

Thank you all so much!"

Ellie told herself they were just saving the telegram for later. *Mrs. Young* did *say no telegrams at school*, she thought.

⋯ ⋯ ⋯ ⋯ ⋯ ⋯ ⋯ ⋯

The girls met up after school at Marion's house. Marion checked

her clipboard. She had the list of addresses they would be going to. "So," said Marion, "there's one very important telegram I think we should deliver first."

Ellie's eyes went wide. *Does she mean my telegram?*

"That's right!" said Amy. Ellie

thought she had a twinkle in her eye. "Ellie, you weren't there yesterday when we talked about this special one."

"Oh? Which one?" Ellie asked. She tried to act natural. But inside she was jumping up and down.

Mine! They must mean mine!

"Ellie, you're going to love this!" said Liz.

I know! I am going to love it! Ellie thought.

Liz went on. "We are delivering another telegram to Grandma Sue—from us this time."

"To give her the good news!" Marion added. "You know, that Princess Boo seems one hundred percent better!"

"My mom agrees," says Amy. "She thinks getting another bird

should do the trick."

Ellie forced a huge smile. "That is a great idea!" she said.

And she *did* think it was a great idea. She was so happy Princess Boo was better. But Ellie couldn't help feeling a pang of jealousy. Grandma Sue was going to get *two* singing telegrams?

Still, Ellie tried to be patient. *Sooner or later, I'll be getting my telegram,* she thought. *Won't I?*

The girls grabbed their coats and the telegrams. Marion led the way toward the garage. Mrs. Ballard

had offered to drive them.

Marion stopped at the garage door. "Oh! I almost forgot," she said. "We're going to sing Grandma Sue's telegram to the tune of 'Take Me Out to the Ballgame.' It seemed to fit well with Amy's words. Plus, we knew you'd know it!"

"It's your favorite song, isn't it?" said Amy.

Ellie nodded while her heart slowly sank. So the girls *had* been talking about her favorite song. But they had been writing a telegram for Grandma Sue—not for her.

"Yes," Ellie said distractedly, as if in a daze. "I do love that song."

But right at that moment, Ellie didn't feel much in the mood to sing it.

Chapter 9

The Last Telegram

"Ta-da!" said Ellie's mom. She put a plate down in the middle of the dining room table. On it were five chocolate-frosted cupcakes with Valentine's Day decorations on top. "Something sweet for my valentines!" said Mrs. Mitchell.

"Yum!" cried Ellie's brother, Toby, reaching for one.

"Thanks, Mom," Ellie added with a little smile as she took one.

Ellie took a bite. The cupcake was so yummy. But Ellie was still feeling blue. She and the girls had had a busy afternoon of delivering telegrams. Delivering Grandma Sue's was especially fun. But now dinner was over and Valentine's Day was almost over too.

Oh, well, she thought. *No singing telegram for me.* Ellie didn't know why she cared so much. She guessed she just wanted to feel special. She tried to cheer herself up by remembering she had done a great thing for Puppy Love.

Ellie was helping her dad clear the dishes when the doorbell rang. She went to answer it.

"Hi, Ellie!" Liz, Marion, and Amy were standing on her front porch. All three were wearing huge grins.

"Hi, you guys," Ellie replied uncertainly. "What's up?"

"Well," said Liz, "we have something for you!"

With that, the three girls started to sing to the tune of "Take Me Out to the Ball Game."

For Ellie!
First you had a great idea.
Then you had a great plan.
We weren't so sure about
singing at school.
You helped us through it
and it turned out cool,
and now Puppy Love pups are smiling.
They want to say something too!
For it's one, two, three,
and they'll
bark out a big
THANK - YOU!

By the end, Ellie was clapping while jumping up and down. "Wow!" she exclaimed. "That was the best! The absolute best!" She hugged each one of them. "You three are the best friends in

the whole wide world!"

Marion laughed. "Thanks, Ellie!"
she said. "We're glad you liked it!"

"But the telegram isn't from us,
you know," Amy added.

Ellie stared. "It's not?"

"Nope," said Liz. She handed Ellie the heart-shaped telegram. On the back, there was a PS.

P.S. Ellie, your fantastic singing telegram idea raised more than $100.⁰⁰ for Puppy Love! Thank you SO much from the puppies and me!
Rebecca

"We raised more than *a hundred dollars?*" cried Ellie. "That's so cool!"

"Yeah, and that's not all," said Amy. She handed Ellie something in a frame.

"Wow! We can hang this at the Critter Club!" Ellie said excitedly.

"And just think of all the pup-pies that will be helped with the

money we raised—from your idea!"
said Liz.

Marion put an arm around Ellie. "We were going to deliver your telegram earlier," she said. "But Rebecca wanted to sign the valentine herself."

Liz smiled. "We were sort of getting the feeling that you'd enjoy a telegram of your own."

Ellie pretended to be confused. "What in the world gave you that idea?" she said. Then she laughed and her friends joined in.

Ellie wasn't sure what was the best: getting a singing telegram, truly helping Puppy Love, or having three best friends who knew her so well.

Suddenly, it felt like the sweetest Valentine's Day ever.

Read on for a sneak peek at
the next Critter Club book:

#7

Liz at Marigold Lake

Squee-onk! Squee-onk! A loud, shrill sound woke Liz Jenkins. *My alarm clock sounds broken,* she thought, only half-awake.

Liz Jenkins rolled over in bed and rubbed her eyes. No, it wasn't her alarm clock! It was a goose honking! Sunlight shone in through the window. Birds chirped outside. It was going to be a beautiful spring day at the cabin.

Liz threw off her flannel sheets and jumped out of bed. "Yes!" she cheered. "It's the perfect weather for the girls' visit!"

Liz's three best friends, Ellie, Marion, and Amy, were coming up to the Jenkins' lake cabin *today* for the three-day weekend. For years, they had heard all about it from Liz. She and her family had been coming to Marigold Lake since Liz was little. But this was the first time Liz had been able to invite her friends.

Liz hurried to change into her clothes. She had lots of things to get ready before the girls arrived. She wanted their first visit to the lake to be perfect.

Out in the cabin's living room, Liz's mom, dad, and big brother, Stewart, were already up.

"Oatmeal in ten minutes, Lizzie!" her dad said.

"Thanks Dad," Liz replied. She was headed for the door. "I'll be back. I just need to do a few things."

Outside, Liz took a deep breath. *Ahhhh. Fresh air.* She smiled at the sight of the big, beautiful lake in the cabin's backyard.

Liz went into the storage shed. She dragged a folded-up tent to a flat area by the campfire pit. "Just the spot," Liz said out loud to herself. She would ask her mom or dad to help her set up the tent later. It was definitely warm enough for the girls to sleep outside in it. Liz couldn't wait to surprise them!

Next, Liz hurried down to the boat dock. She took the tarp off the red canoe and made sure the life jackets were there. *We can paddle around the whole lake*, she thought.

Then, on her way back to the cabin, Liz picked up every long, thin stick she saw. *We're* definitely *roasting marshmallows over a camp-fire*, she decided. She left her pile of roasting sticks next to the camp-fire pit.

Liz stopped to think. Canoeing, swimming, camping out, marsh-mallow-roasting, plus hiking on the nature path . . .

I hope we have time for every-thing! she thought excitedly.

If you like **the CRiTTeR club** you'll love **HEiDi HECKELBECK**